Claimed by the Mountain Man – A Short, Steamy Grumpy-Sunshine Mountain Man Romance

By Ann Ric

Mountain Men of Charming Falls

Books by Ann Ric

Mountain Men of Charming Falls

Rescued by the Mountain Man (Evie & Jake)
Claimed by the Mountain Man (Candi & Erik)
Stranded with the Mountain Man (Lilly & Alex)
Christmas with the Mountain Man (Harmony & Chase)

Magic Protector Reverse Harem Trilogy

Magic Protector – A Steamy Paranormal Reverse Harem Romance (Book 1)
Magic Bound – A Steamy Paranormal Reverse Harem Romance (Book 2)
Magic Promise – A Steamy Paranormal Reverse Harem Romance (Book 3)

Claimed by the Mountain Man

A sweet, grumpy ex-military mountain man and a shy, curvy wedding floral arranger. An undeniable chemistry. Can love bring them together?

When Candi, a talented floral designer who makes floral arrangements for lonely patients or deserving brides on a budget, finds herself lost on the mountains without cell phone service on her way to her friend's wedding, she knows she's in trouble…

Until she's rescued by a gorgeous mountain man with biceps of steel and a sweet, grumpy demeanor. Should she trust her heart around this handsome recluse?

Welcome to ***Mountain Men of Charming Falls***, the spicy instalove series based on a picturesque small mountain town by a lake that brings you closer to nature. A tranquil scenic escape from the busy city where residents in the cozy close-knit community look out for each other. Let the cool mountain breeze, clear night skies, beautiful romantic sunsets, and the fresh pine scents that fill the air bring you serene relaxation. Known for its camping sites, rustic cabin retreats, hiking trails, ski slopes, and yes, semi-recluse hot and sexy ex-military mountain men who live by the honor code: respect, loyalty, selfless service, integrity and courage in everything they do. Charming Falls is the perfect place to fall in love.

Chapter 1 - Candi

Candi's Boyfriend Wish List

1. *A guy who understands me and appreciates me*

2. *A guy who loves flowers*

3. *A guy who's a great kisser and yes, great in bed*

4. *A guy who shares a lot in common with me*

5. *A guy who is sexy and charming*

6. *A guy who is faithful and honest*

7. *A guy who wants to commit to a long-term relationship—yes, marriage one day*

The Boyfriend Wish List or Soul Mate Wish List was going viral now on social media and Candi had decided to post her own list—for fun, of course. It wasn't like she'd ever find a guy who ticked all the right boxes.

Candi packed items into her car for her new gig, thinking about her wish list. It had been a fun experience creating the list.

She followed an old school friend of hers who had a popular blog about weddings and all things romance. It gave her a chance to look at what she desired in a soul mate and what *she* could give to a relationship too. Sometimes it's good to know what you want in life. Or at least dream about it.

Right now, Candi was living a small part of her dream. Creating special arrangements for deserving brides-to-be. Many of the brides that came to her small company were women who'd lost everything during a catastrophic event like a hurricane or other natural disaster and wanted to start their life over. She donated most of her arrangements.

Candi also made flowers for patients at her local hospital in New York who didn't get many visitors. It was her own way of giving back to her community while bringing a smile to someone's face. Right now, she was happy to provide the flowers for her other friend, Cat's wedding. Cat was short for Catherine.

Candi wanted to help make this a special day for Cat. She deserved it. Cat had lost her home during the last hurricane and was looking forward to rebuilding her life with her new groom-to-be.

Candi had always been involved in weddings—just not her own. She loved to create and provide the pretty floral arrangements and of course, the bridal bouquet for the woman of the day. That's why she opened up *Candi's Bridal Bouquet & Floral Arrangements* after college when she was trying to figure out what type of business she wanted to run.

She loved bridal bouquets because they symbolized hope and new beginnings. In fact, in ancient Egypt, bridal bouquets were not only carried for the fragrance from the collection of flowers, but for the idea that they could ward off bad luck during the bride's wedding. She wished it worked for those *making* the arrangements too.

She loved watching her friends get married, but deep down inside, Candi knew she wasn't getting any younger and couldn't help but think that maybe she would never have that happily ever after one day.

Candi thought she had it with her ex, but she wasn't good enough for him according to his actions. He'd always criticized her weight and her curves that went on forever. He ended up leaving her for an aspiring size-one model, a cheerleader. Well, good for them.

She was going to be providing all the flowers for her friend Cat's wedding to Carter Heat. Cat deserved to be happy and she couldn't be more thrilled that she was with a really nice guy. One of the Heat brothers from Charming Falls. The once sworn bachelor.

She'd heard that all the brothers, who'd all served overseas at one time or another, had made a pact to never settle down or get married. She was happily surprised Carter had changed his mind. How did she get him to change his mind?

Love could make anything happen.

Would Candi ever get so lucky in love? When she thought about her own love life, it made her shake her head.

Her ex kept telling her to lose weight or go on a diet. Like that would make her as thin as a toothpick. She realized she was a big-boned girl and yes, she loved food, but no matter how much she tried, she would never be as thin as a coat hanger. She was who she was. He didn't accept that and left her for one of the cheerleaders at their college. Well, that was three years ago. Her self-esteem had taken a hit since then. But she was determined to build herself up again and focus on her career.

It had been three years since she'd last dated.

Three years since her ex left her for another girl.

She'd begun to feel self-conscious about dating and didn't want any guy to make her feel the way her ex did ever again. Right now, her heart was closed for a break—taking a long holiday.

If she couldn't walk down the aisle then she'd make sure every girl who did had the most beautiful day ever!

Just then her phone rang.

It was Cat.

"Hey, bride-to-be? How are you? Nervous?" she teased her friend.

Candi met Cat when Cat moved from her hometown of Charming Falls to New York to share an apartment with Candi. Since then Cat had moved back to her hometown.

"Not nervous enough," Cat said. "Thanks so much for doing my flowers."

"Hey, you know I've got your back. Besides, who else would you want to go to for your flowers, girl?"

Cat laughed. "Do you want me to get one of Carter's brothers to pick you up from the airport?"

"Oh, no. I'm not flying. In fact, I'll be driving there."

"Candi, that's a long trip. Are you sure you're okay to do that?"

"Course, I'm okay. Where are you?"

"At the salon getting my hair done."

"Good for you. I'll see you later, okay."

"Okay, just call me if you need anything. Thanks again. You're a gem."

Candi smiled after her call as she put the finishing touches on Cat's 12-stem champagne and pink colored silk peony roses bouquet with eucalyptus leaves. Her most requested design.

Most brides preferred artificial flowers for their bouquets instead of real ones, but Candi used beautiful custom-made silk flowers that looked real and they were in demand compared to fresh flowers, and more durable.

This also helped brides who were allergic to flowers. She had them packed in her car and ready for her road trip out of state to the small mountain town of Charming Falls.

***

Later, Candi drove along the country road after entering the town of Charming Falls, population 7,000. It was a quaint small town by the lake with amazing mountains. She loved the change from the big city with all the traffic and noise. The sun was beginning to set in the west. It gave the town a more romantic glow. Always the romantic at heart, her ex never cared for stuff like that. Sunsets and watching the stars at night. He thought she was crazy to even sit out watching the sunset. So much for having anything in common.

Just as Candi was about to turn on Cedar Lane through the wooded area, she heard a very strange hissing sound coming from the hood of her car.

"Oh, no. Oh, no, no, no." This could not be happening now. The wedding was in two days and the rehearsal was for tomorrow. She needed to have the flowers at Cat's place tonight. What was she going to do?

She turned off the ignition and reached into her handbag for her phone.

It wasn't there.

Where was her phone?

Her heart leaped in her chest as panic consumed her.

She was lost without her cell phone. It was like walking around without her head on. Her cell phone was everything! Her contacts, her pictured memories, her favorite songs, all her books, her GPS, her search engine, her security, her flashlight, her companion on long road trips when making out of town deliveries, her only way of communicating with others when she was outside the home.

She felt naked without her phone.

She turned the bag upside down and fished around for it.

Nothing.

Her heart thumped hard in her chest. The hairs on her neck stood up.

She was in the middle of nowhere without a phone!

"What the…"

Did she leave her phone in New York? Did it slide out of her handbag when she gathered the boxes to put into the trunk of her car?

She was so lost without her cell. She felt naked without it.

Oh, no. Now she remembered. She was helping her neighbor Mr. Darnel tie his shoe laces. He was a nice older man but he looked as if he was going to trip on his laces. She remembered kneeling down with her bag slung over her shoulder, it could have fallen out then but she didn't hear a thumping sound on the ground.

It was so noisy out on the street when she saw him. It could have hit the pavement and she didn't hear it.

Great, now she had to call the phone company to cancel the service in case anyone ran up her phone bill.

This was so *not* how she envisioned her weekend.

What was she going to do now? Her car was down. She was in the wooded area of Charming Falls with no cell phone service. She was in trouble.

Chapter 2 - Erik

Erik grabbed the wedding invitation from the side table in his cabin and read it again.

He was happy his half-brother was getting married. But he had no intention of going to the wedding. He hoped his bro would understand. He hadn't been that close to the family since a rift tore them further apart. And quite frankly, he preferred living away from everyone. Besides the occasional drink with his army buddies after a long day of volunteering his time in the community repairing rooftops, he spent most of his time in his cabin on the mountains.

That's why he built it. After that fateful night years ago, it was all for the best.

Like many of his army buddies, Erik had struggled to cope with life after the war and fitting back into society. He'd found solace in helping others who've been through turmoil and spending the rest of his free time meditating on the mountains.

Erik placed the invitation down.

He then grabbed his keys and headed out into town to pick up some more firewood.

He drove down the gravel road of Second Chance Lane – one of the longest dirt roads on the mountains that housed many secluded cabins. It was then that he saw her…

A woman. Not just any woman. A beautiful woman with curves in all the right places. She had gorgeous wavy hair that ran down her shoulders. Her skin looked soft. And those lips. Her lips were shapely and looked kissable. He envisioned himself wrapping his arms around her waist and bringing her to him.

What was wrong with him? He had to get a hold of himself, he thought as he got out of his SUV and neared the curvy princess in distress.

Wait a minute. That wasn't just any beautiful girl. It was Candi…or was it Camry. He wasn't great with names. Just pretty faces. And one like this woman he'd never forget. She was a friend of Cat. He saw her a couple times at the town's annual barbecue, whenever he did attend. He'd admired her from afar. But right now she was closer to him.

"You all right, Miss?" he asked, not wanting to get her name wrong.

He realized his voice was loud and sounded hard and he hoped he wouldn't frighten her.

"Hi," she said. "Could be better. Oh, you're Carter's brother," she said, recognizing him. She bounced a couple times on the spot with joy—this darling Ms Sunshine seemed happy to see him. She probably forgot his name just as he'd forgotten hers. It's been over a year since they'd met after all.

Even her voice sounded angelic. Erik had never felt that kind of instant reaction to a woman before. And this woman was lovely. Sure, he'd heard about love at first sight. But he never thought it would happen to him. He never believed it was even possible.

"Your car?" he said.

"Yeah, it died on me," she said, in a sing-song voice. "Picked a great location to do it too." She was funny with an optimistic vibe about her. She was like a breath a fresh air. He liked that about her. So unlike many of the women he'd met.

"Yeah, that always happens, doesn't it?" he agreed.

She grinned.

"I'm Erik."

"Hi Erik. I remember you." Her face lit up. "I'm Candi with an I."

Candi. That's right. Even her name sounded as sweet as she looked. This was one candy he would love to lick from top to curvy bottom before thrusting deep inside her. Okay, he had to get his mind away from any dirty thoughts. Why was he going there all of a sudden. It had been a while since he'd been with a woman but he still never got that kind of reaction before.

"Candi with an I. Nice to see you again. I can take a look at it for you."

'Thanks. I'm supposed to be at Cat's wedding in two days."

He paused for a moment.

Charming Falls was a small town. Almost everybody knew each other. Of course she was going to his brother's wedding. The bride-to-be was her friend.

Surprise filled her lovely oval-shaped face. Or was that relief.

"I'm so glad to meet you now at a time like this," she said, bubbly. "Thank you for doing this?"

"Hey, anything for a beautiful lady like you."

Her skin flushed.

"Hope to see you at the wedding," she said. She probably heard about the fall out with the family. He barely went around them these days. He liked to keep to himself.

He loved the way her breasts moved when she bobbed up a moment ago with excitement. He wanted to bury himself in her, in between her.

She was his brother's bride's best friend. This could only get complicated. He promised himself after his ex left that he'd never date anyone his family knew. It got ugly. They all took his ex's side. Even though his ex was the one that had cheated on him. So, he wasn't a guy that expressed himself much. But that didn't give her the right to betray him. His ex and he had nothing in common.

It always got messy when family got into your personal business. He vowed never again. But here he was—again with someone close to his family.

Just then, a hissing sound came from the car.

Good. A distraction.

He popped the hood open of her car and took a look.

"Is it as bad as it sounds?" she asked, hugging herself. Something *he* wanted to do to her. Just to wrap his arms around her and let her know everything was going to be okay.

"The coolant's leaking on the exhaust," he told her. "I'll make sure that's taken care of for you," he reassured.

"Thank you. How will I ever repay you?"

Just then his cock jumped. Desire rushed through him, thinking of how he'd love to repay her for the feeling he was having throughout his body. Man, he needed a cold shower. He needed to get his mind out of that place.

"Don't worry about it," he just said. "You want to call Cat and let her know you'll be late?"

"I just realized I don't have my cell phone. I must have left in in New York."

"Ouch. That's not good. Here, use mine." He pulled out his cell phone from his pocket and handed it to her.

"Thanks."

Their hands brushed and a light feeling swept through his belly. It was like magic. Her touch was so smooth, delicate. He wondered if she felt it too.

He noticed a box of flowers in the back seat of her car.

"Peony roses with eucalyptus leaves," he observed. "Nice selection. Are those for the wedding?"

"Yes, I made them. I specialize in flowers to make life beautiful for the receiver."

"I like that."

A pretty woman who's an entrepreneur and loved beautiful things in life, like making life beautiful for others. She was sweet, just like her name.

She seemed surprised by his reaction. He saw her lovely shapely kissable-looking lips curve into a wide smile. He wanted nothing more than to reach out and brush his lips over hers. But he had to contain himself and get his mind as far away from her tempting lips as possible.

"I can't believe you know your flowers," she said, shaking her head in wonder. "I mean most guys don't know anything about plants outside of red roses."

"Hey, I live out in the woods. It's good to know what's poisonous and what's not." He grinned.

She laughed heartily in response.

The sweet sound coming from her lips sounded like melody to his ears. Her laugh was beautifully contagious and warm. He remembered from the last time he'd met her briefly at the community barbecue. She seemed like a pure joy to be around. He wondered if she was seeing anyone.

She was a world apart from his ex. Talk about differences. His ex never appreciated anything in life. And especially him. His ex was more materialistic and scheming. She'd been playing him while seeing someone else.

His ex was the reason he'd stopped believing in love or in good people. But this Candi was…well, she was like a breath of fresh mountain air. Did the universe bring her into his path to let him know that there was a good woman for him.

Wait a minute. He was getting way ahead of himself.

He watched surreptitiously from the corner of his eyes as she made the call. He loved the way her ass moved as she walked a few steps away for privacy. What he'd love to do that woman. Pleasure her in ways she'd never forget.

"You just know," his grandfather once told him. *"When you meet the one who makes your heart go in places it's never been before. That's the one. Your heart just knows. It could happen when you least expect it."*

Was his grandfather right?

As Candi spoke to her friend Cat, Erik's future sister-in-law, she glanced up in Erik's direction every now and then.

He grinned to himself, arching a brow.

Were they talking about him?

While he continued to look under the hood of her car, making sure there was nothing else serious, he couldn't help but feel something for this pretty curvy girl near to him.

When Candi got off the phone she said, "My friend thinks the world of you. Well, at least I know I'm in good hands."

"Glad you think so. Can't be too careful talking to strangers."

"Well, you're hardly a stranger now, are you? We're going to be like in laws."

"In laws? I thought you said Cat was your friend."

"Well, yes. But we're practically sisters. We're really close. She told me her fiancé had a lot of brothers. And that you're all a tight family. A good family."

"So you've vetted me. Good for you. Now let's get your car taken care of. I'll get my men at the shop to check it out. It should be up and running in no time."

Her face fell.

Did he say something wrong?

Chapter 3 – Candi

What had gotten into Candi all of a sudden? Her pulse pounded in her veins. Her heart jolted with excitement. She couldn't remember the last time she'd had that kind of reaction to a guy. Oh, wait. It was the last time she saw this handsome mountain man, Erik. Waves of excitement swept through her body when her rescuer this afternoon turned out to be Erik.

She'd had a crush on him from the last time she visited Charming Falls but since she was still nursing a broken heart when she first met Erik over a year ago, she never acted on it. She didn't even mention it to her friend. She just kept those feelings bottled up inside.

Her eyes drank in his stunning physique. Erik was muscular-built with a nice beard and sinfully sexy. The color of his blue eyes resembled a cloudless blue sky. She was mesmerized by him. He was so different from her ex in many ways. Her body was turned on by seeing him again. She'd never felt this way about her ex.

Her heart thumped hard in her chest when he neared her. Her inner thighs tingled with pleasure earlier when he'd brushed his skin over hers as he handed her his phone before going to look under the hood of her car. Funny how her ex didn't know anything about cars. Not that she expected all guys to. But she knew ex-military soldiers were good at a lot of things. Plus she'd heard from Cat that Erik's huge size and bulging muscles didn't sum him up—he could be unsmiling and grumpy at times but underneath all that, he had a huge heart. He was protective of those close to him. Even if they weren't on speaking terms. She'd heard that he had a falling out with some of his brothers but when they'd had trouble in town, he was there for them at their side as if nothing happened between them.

He was polite and kind and had the most beautiful eyes she'd ever seen on a guy. And he was so helpful.

Okay, he definitely got a check mark for item number five on her boyfriend wish list. Erik was sexy *and* charming. She could not tear her eyes away from this gorgeous rough-around-the-edges mountain man. Wasn't that what they were called? Men who lived up on the mountain in a cabin. Either way, she felt something for him.

And she couldn't forget Boyfriend Wish List item #2.

Erik. Loved. Flowers.

He not only appreciated her passion in life, but he *knew* flowers. Was this a dream or what?

They were so connected in so many ways. She could not believe he identified her selection of peony roses and eucalyptus leaves.

It took a lot to impress Candi. And she was impressed with Erik.

Most people didn't even know what her flowers were called. A smile warmed her soul. She felt a sweet chemistry and understanding between them. She hoped it wasn't just one-sided. Was he charming to all the women he met?

Stop thinking negative, Candi.
Think positive for a change.

Okay, she was going to be thinking positive from now on. They hung out in the same circles, right? And right now, she positively wanted to be with this guy from the mountains of Charming Falls.

She did not want to leave him. She wanted to know more about this Erik guy. Her friend Cat told her that he lived in the wooded area of Charming Falls. Away from everyone. Yes, she managed to get a bit of background info on this guy. And she wanted more.

Just then, thunder sounded in the sky.

"Oh, no," she said.

"What's wrong?" he asked.

"Oh, nothing. It's just that…" She screamed out when a large roll of thunder sounded and light flashed in the now darkening sky.

"You okay?" he said, probably noticing that her body tensed. He noticed. Her ex never noticed anything about her. She could be drowning right beside her ex and he wouldn't even notice.

"I'm okay."

"You don't look okay. Don't worry, I won't let anything happen to you." His voice was commanding, strong and sincere.

"Thank you." Relief washed over her that she was in Erik's company.

"Come let me take you to Cat's house. That's where you're headed right?"

She wished he was taking her to *his* cabin.

Why couldn't he take her to his cabin instead?

Wait. What the heck was going on with her? Ordinarily she would never think of going to a guy's home alone. Not a guy she'd just met a few times. Although they knew the same people. And the Heat brothers have a good reputation in this mountain town. They were honorable ex-military soldiers who gave back to their community. That's what she'd heard from her sisterly friend Cat.

Thunder rolled louder in the sky and the dark clouds immediately covered them. The blue sky had vanished.

Erik made a phone call to one of his workers to get Candi's car towed to his garage. After he finished his call, he turned to Candi.

"You can sit in my ride while I get the flowers out of your backseat."

"Thank you, Erik," she said as rain started to pour down instantly.

She watched from the passenger side seat in his very clean SUV as he gathered her flowers carefully and then placed them in the back seat of his vehicle. He then went back to her car to make sure the doors were locked.

As the rain continued, she couldn't help but noticed his bulging muscles and wet skin. Her inner thighs tingled with delight. There was something sexy about wet muscles on a gorgeous sculptured guy.

Erik. Was. Sexy.

"I'll drive you to Cat's house," he said as he got back into his SUV and slammed the door shut. The rain pounded the ground outside, visibility had decreased. Talk about raining cats and dogs out there.

Disappointment flooded through her like the rain pouring down. She was hoping to spend more time with Erik this afternoon. Not that she didn't want to see her friend Cat. She just loved the way she felt around him.

She noticed the way his lovely blue eyes surveyed her body with delight, a grin of approval curved his sexy lips. Yes, that's right. Unlike the way her ex used to look with disgust at her curves and her not-flat belly. Erik had briefly roamed his eyes over her with a look of genuine appreciation and admiration. The men she'd met in the past weren't really like that. They'd preferred skinny girls. Clearly, Erik was not like any other guy she'd ever met. Though she'd only really had one boyfriend.

Candi was good at picking up on vibes from others. And Erik was sending her nothing but good, sweet vibes.

"How can I ever repay you?" she said, biting down on her lower lip.

She noticed his gaze fell to her lips. Was that hunger in his eyes? He then shifted his focus, looking out the windshield as the rain pummeled down.

"Just take care of yourself." His voice was deep and sexy to her ears.

Just then a call came in on his phone. He answered it before driving out. When he finished, he said, "Bad news."

"Bad news? Oh, no. What's wrong?"

"There's a pile up near River Road. Truck collided on the road. Don't know if there are any injuries. Hope not. But that way is blocked. We won't be able to make it out there to Cat's. That's the only way to her place."

"Oh, no. I hope this weather lets up soon."

"Charming Falls is known for its turbulent rainy season as much as it's snowy winters."

"Charming."

"You can come up to my cabin and we can wait it out there until the storm lets up. Not safe to be out on the road right now anyway," he said in his deep voice, his expression serious.

Her breath caught in her throat. She wanted nothing more than to be alone with Erik. And now it looked as if the universe was going to answer her silent wish.

But the trouble was, could she handle being alone with Erik—in his cabin on the mountain?

She had to think straight.

"That okay with you?" he asked her.

"Sure. I'd…." She didn't want to sound too eager. She was about to say she'd like that, but instead she said. "Why not? I just hope I'm not going to inconvenience you."

She figured he wasn't expecting any guests and probably liked being alone. Was he just being kind? She had no idea, but oh, her body was saying something entirely different. Her nipples tightened under her T-shirt when he brushed his hand over hers earlier. The energy in his vehicle was pulsating. She felt warm inside being near Erik.

The sweet spicy scent of his cologne wafted to her nostrils as they sat in his vehicle while the rainfall pummeled the windshield as if they were driving through a car wash. But right now, she felt as if she was going through the wash with her emotions. She was supposed to be on a break from men right now. But why, oh, why was she picturing herself pleasuring Erik up in his cabin, running her tongue over his erection and then sucking and taking him in deeply. He was an enormous man and salivated wondering how huge his cock was.

Stop that, Candi. You're on a break from men now, remember? Focus, girl. Just focus on your floral business and your future. Even if Erik does tick a lot of boxes

"It's about a ten-minute drive up the road there," he said interrupting her thoughts as he started up his engine.

And the engine of his SUV wasn't the only thing to be turned on right now.

She really had to get her mind to another place. This could only spell trouble—being stuck in a cabin on the mountain in Charming Falls with a strikingly good-looking physically fit mountain man.

Yep, her friend Cat already told her about Charming Falls, the place where people fell in love because the men were all so damn sexy and charming as hell. Well, now she was beginning to feel that but she had to control herself. And that was not going to be easy.

"Good. I'm glad it's not far," she said.

Inside, she half-wished it were far so she could cool herself down, but then again maybe being in the confined space in his truck wouldn't help. Things just might get a lot more heated between them.

Chapter 4 – Erik

What was with Erik?

He never got this close to anyone before. But he had an overwhelming urge to claim this lovely curvy princess and take good care of her, cherish her body and her soul. To protect her.

After he'd come back from his last tour of duty he'd worked in toxic work environments where everybody had an agenda. Everyone was standoffish— including his ex, someone he'd met at his previous job.

But not Candi.

She was as sweet as her name sounded. Sweet on the inside and outside. He remembered from the last time he'd met her briefly at the community barbecue.

A surge of desire rushed through his groin. Candi had an instant effect on him.

He wasn't a man who smiled often but something inside Candi brought out something inside him. Her glowing complexion and infectious smile and honey vibes made him feel warm inside. She had an air of innocence around her aura.

He'd sworn he'd never get into a relationship again. He'd built a wall around his heart after his ex had cheated on him.

Was Candi melting his defenses?

He often kept his distance from others.

And it wasn't just friends and co-workers. He kept his distance from his own family too. But he felt something strange around Candi. He felt his dick harden and his heart soften around her. She radiated honesty, frankness, and sincerity.

She wasn't afraid to say what was on her mind. There was no guessing with her.

And she appreciated that he loved flowers.

Doing a bit of gardening was the only thing that seemed to calm him these days. His ex thought he was too soft inside when she got to know him. His ex wanted a man that was all macho twenty-four-seven and rough around the edges but Erik was not like that behind closed doors. She never liked a man with an easy-going side. He had no trouble defending his country and putting his life on the front line for others but deep down, he hid the fact that he wasn't a guy that wanted to harm anyone.

Candi seemed to appreciate his love of flowers. He felt he could be himself around her and she wouldn't ridicule him or belittle him or comment on how hard he looked on the outside yet gentle inside.

He had a soft spot while growing up but after being teased and bullied for it, he'd learned to fight and defend himself. He'd always kept a wall up around his heart and his feelings. He never liked getting close to anyone before.

But he felt different around sweet Candi.

Still, he had to take it slow. He was growing attracted to her but he didn't want to frighten her off.

Chapter 5 – Candi

Before long, they reached Erik's cozy cabin on the mountain with a breathtaking view. The scenery was impressive. The rain came down harder though and she was getting drenched as much as he tried to shield her from the rain with the jacket he took off and held over her. She appreciated his chivalry.

They walked up the steps from his SUV to the pathway leading to the cabin. She tried hard to steer her eyes away from his ripped muscles bulging as his wet shirt clung to his skin.

"Thank you for doing this for me," she said as they stepped inside his cozy digs, hugging herself.

Her pussy throbbed with arousal and desire as she eyed his bulging muscles and his taut nipples through his wet shirt. Oh, man, he looked hot. He was ripped in all the right places. She fought hard not to ogle him. She felt heat climb to her cheeks and was sure she was blushing.

Did he realize how stunningly gorgeous he was?

"Hey, glad I could help you," he said, without smiling.

Ever since she met him last year, she'd never seen him smile. Like ever. He always had this serious look on his face, yet she saw undeniable kindness in his beautiful blue eyes framed with long thick dark lashes.

It was as if he was against smiling or showing his true feelings. It was as if he was hiding behind a wall.

Was it a wall of hurt or pain? A wall of a broken heart?

She wondered, silently. Her spirit drawn to this gentle giant. Well, she certainly knew a thing or two about having a broken heart.

"So you're going to my brother's wedding," he said when they stepped inside his log cabin.

She was surprised at the beautiful surroundings of his rustic charming dwelling. It was clean and had a fresh scent about. She noticed he had some plants beautifully placed throughout his cabin.

Very charming. She did not expect to see that coming from an ex-military mountain man. He seemed to appreciate nature and beautiful things.

"Yes, what a coincidence," she replied, swallowing a nervous lump in her throat.

"It sure is."

"By the way, you have a cozy home," she said, noticing the polished hardwood floors.

"Thanks. It's a place to lay my head."

"Well, it's a *lovely* place to lay your head."

And she would love to lay *her* head down with him too.

Okay, enough naughty thoughts, Candi.

It seemed as if being celibate these past few years had done a number on her hormones. But even so, she'd seen guys at her building but never felt any sort of attraction to them—not like this.

"I guess you'll be busy soon, with the wedding," she said.

"I'm not going." His shapely lips were pinched into a thin line.

She was stunned into silence.

"You're not going? Why not?"

He said nothing for a moment.

"It's complicated," he finally said, sighing.

She didn't want to push him further but she was disappointed she wouldn't be seeing him there.

"These flowers are really pretty," he said, changing the subject as he lay her boxes of floral designs down. "Love your arrangement. You're so creative."

She beamed, excitement rose in her chest. "Thank you. Most guys don't talk about stuff like that."

"Why not? You need to tell me how you got started at dinner."

She could not believe he was so interested in that. And dinner. Was he going to fix her dinner too?

"Speaking of arrangements, I love the flowers and plants you have in your cabin," she commented. She noticed there wasn't any family photos or anything like that.

"Thanks. You'd better get into something dry," he said immediately. His voice was so deep and sexy, she was immediately drawn to him.

No, Candi. No. Focus. You're supposed to be focusing on flower beds, not Erik's bed. Not right now.

But why on earth was she so drawn to him?

"I have a shirt you can wear. It's long enough to um…cover you up. Should come to below your knees."

"Sure, that would be fine," she said.

"You can change in my room. I'll get your clothes washed and dried."

"You have a washing machine here?"

"Of course. Energy efficient too. And a low energy dryer. It shouldn't take too long to dry."

"Thank you for doing this for me. I really appreciate it. I hope I'm not putting you out."

"With the weather like this, I didn't have much planned, so it's cool. Besides, it's nice to catch up since we last met."

"Right. Of course."

Her heart thumped hard and fast in her chest.

She'd had a crush on him when she met him last year at the Charming Falls community barbecue.

He was so cute, yet distant. She never got a chance to speak to him much then. She was relieved she'd met him while stuck on the mountain and not someone else.

The scent of his sweet earthy cologne wafted to her nostrils again and she found him irresistible. She tried to shift her focus though.

Before long, he'd showed her into his room where he pulled out a clean pressed long plaid shirt for her to wear.

"I…um…I can get your clothes washed for you," he said, nervously combing his fingers through his thick dark hair then stroking his beard. "You can leave them outside the door. I'll get dinner ready now. You like broiled chicken and rice."

"Yes, I do. Thanks."

There was a brief moment when their gaze locked and she saw something sweet in his beautiful blue eyes, then he turned away and left the room so that she could undress and change into something clean and dry.

Before long, she was in Erik's red plaid shirt which felt soft against her skin, imagining what it would feel like to have Erik on her skin instead.

Why did that naughty thought slide into her mind?

She really appreciated that Erik was a sweet and gentle giant. He never tried to take advantage of her in any way, especially knowing she was in nothing but his shirt while he washed and dried her clothes.

Before long, dinner was heated up.

"*Mmm*, this is delicious," she said to him.

"Thanks," he said, not smiling. His voice was warm but his expression was unreadable.

Later, she spoke about what drew her to creating pretty wedding flowers, how much she loved them and wanted to experience that one day too.

They got to talking about all kinds of cool stuff.

She found out they had so much in common. They both loved to give back to their community. He seemed genuinely interested in her work in delivering flowers to lonely patients and for making floral arrangements for deserving brides.

She was impressed with his work in volunteering his time and skills in repairing the roof tops of damaged homes from storms or other disasters.

And he was witty and charming. Guarded about his heart too. She'd learned that his ex had crushed his heart and there was a terrible accident in which she later died—with her lover.

It shook him up. It wasn't his fault. He wasn't even there, but he felt guilty he wasn't there to save her. Her heart ached for him. What a burden to carry and it wasn't even his fault. And she was with another man.

Still, she learned Erik's family had liked his late ex. A lot. But that was all in the past now.

He told her he spent most of his time alone.

Yet right now, he seemed so interested in Candi's life.

Her ex couldn't really care less about her dreams. Erik was fascinated by them. She loved that he was interested in her likes and dislikes, her business.

And speaking of business. She'd vowed to stay focused on it for now and cool off dating after her ex broke her heart to pieces.

Later after dinner, she noticed Erik's eyes drawn to hers.

"What? Something wrong?" she asked.

"Oh, no. I've never met anyone so beautiful." He paused, then said. "I'm sorry, I shouldn't have said that."

"Oh, no, it's okay." Heat climbed to her cheeks. "Thank you," she said, her voice more sensuous than she'd intended.

A grin curved his sweet sexy lips. That was the first time she'd seen him smile. And man, he was gorgeous. He had a lovely smile. And his lips were perfectly shaped.

"What's so funny," he said.

"Nothing. I just thought the same about you. I mean sexy. Never met a guy so sexy before and…"

They both got up from the table.

"I'll clean up. You can relax," he said.

"Oh, no. You made dinner. It's only fair that I help out with the dishes."

"But you're my guest," he said.

Just then a loud roll of thunder crashed down and she leaped into his arms.

"Oh, no. Sorry. I'm so sorry," she breathed. And as she inhaled, his sensuous cologne drove her wild. His strong arms around her melted her inside.

"It's okay, beautiful. It's just a bit of noise," he said, gently and waves of desire for him coursed through her. "I'm right here." His tone was so reassuring.

"I'm sorry," she said.

"Don't be. Nothing to be sorry about." Oh, she loved the low pitch of his deep voice, so relaxing, so sensuous.

She felt genuine care radiating from him. He didn't think she was strange at all.

She looked up into his beautiful eyes and pressed her lips to his, capturing him. His lips felt soft and lovely. She tingled with delight inside.

He kissed her back, devouring her, passionately. She'd never been kissed like *that* before. Ever. And it was breathtaking. Sensuous. Delight slid down her spine and through her belly.

He stopped, leaving her breathless, wanting more. She could hear her own heartbeat.

"Why did you stop?"

"Because I want you, Candi. I liked you from the moment I first met you last year. But I don't want to rush you. Or rush into things."

"I…" Candi was speechless for the first time in her life. What was she going to say? That he could rush her all he wanted? Of course not.

"You know something, I like you too. From the moment we first met at that barbecue last year. I've never done anything like this before. I want to be with you tonight. This is so unlike me but you know what…I want this. Just one night."

"Listen," he said breathing hard. "I don't know if this would be a good idea."

"And why not? I had an instant attraction to you for over a year since I last saw you and I never acted on it. It's a year later and I still have that feeling for you."

He grinned. "I have the same feeling," he said, in his low husky deep voice.

Her eyes were drawn to the huge bulge in his pants and she salivated. Wanting every inch of him inside her soon.

His erection was practically straining to be free.

"I feel as if I've known you forever," she murmured between sweet kisses. "And trust me, I'm not a girl that moves fast. *At all.*" She emphasized the last part.

She sucked in a deep breath. "I've decided I want to try something new."

"What do you mean by that, beautiful?" he said, stroking her cheek, looking into her eyes. Butterflies exploded in her belly.

"The girl I was before I met you was a different girl. I used to worry about everything. Take my time ultra-slow. Calculate everything. Overthink everything. Analyse everything."

"What's wrong with doing all of that? You can't be too careful in this crazy world, you know. I'm a guy that would never hurt a girl. Ever. But not all guys are like that."

"I appreciate that. And thanks for being honest. But that's just it. I ended up with the wrong guy even though I took it slow and did all the right things. I think I'll do something different. Someone once said if you keep getting the same results try something new."

A sexy grin curved his sweet lips. She wanted to melt into him.

Chapter 6 – Candi

Electricity sparked between them. Candi didn't know what got into her all of a sudden. Desire for Erik coursed through her veins. She'd never felt this instant attraction to anyone before. Ever. Not like this.

She'd always been afraid to act on her feelings. But where had that gotten her? Right now, she wanted sweet, honorable Erik.

He wasn't boastful like her ex, just a misunderstood mountain man who didn't mess around and liked to keep to himself. But there was something inside her that was drawn to him.

She could feel that magnetic chemistry between them.

"Oh, Candi, I want you," he groaned, inching closer to her. The scent of his delicious cologne wafted to her nostrils. He was irresistible.

"I want you too," she whispered, hearing the loud pounding of her own heartbeat. She wrapped her arms around the back of Erik's neck, wanting him to take her right there, right then.

He leaned down and pressed his sweet, soft lips to hers.

This man could sure kiss.

She loved the taste of his lips, the feel of his soft tongue sliding in between her lips. Her pussy throbbed with want for him.

"Oh, Candi," he groaned with pleasure.

She could feel the hard erection straining behind his pants as he leaned into her.

"You want to go into the bedroom," he said, between passionate kisses as his lips seared a path down her neck.

The feel of his lips on her neck sent her senses into overload. She loved the sensation and yet he hadn't even been inside her yet. This man's touch was so magical. She felt his energy, his passion towards her.

"No, here's fine," she said. "I want you now," she moaned, not wanting to stop.

"You have the finest body I've ever seen," he said, admiration in his eyes.

"Thank you. My ex told me I was a little too heavy."

"Are you kidding me. You're perfect. I love your curves; I love everything about you Candi."

No one had ever said that to her before. Delight filled her, butterflies tickled her tummy. She loved how she felt around Erik. She adored the way he gazed lovingly into her eyes. She craved everything about him.

She loved the look of desire in his sexy blue eyes as he captured her gaze with his. Appreciation filled his eyes as he surveyed her body.

Her hands slid up and down his hard muscular biceps. Gosh, he was so fit. She couldn't wait to feel him all over her.

He brushed his lips over her skin again sending waves of pleasure through her body as he carefully slid off the shirt she was wearing. She had nothing else underneath.

"You are so beautiful," he said, admiring her body. A grin of approval curved his soft lips. "You have no idea what you do to me," he groaned.

"Take me," she said, seductively.

He slid his fingers over her folds and she quivered in delight.

"You're so wet," he moaned into her neck. She loved the feel of the warm breath on her skin. "I want to fuck you so badly, beautiful," he said. "I want to be inside you."

That did it. Her pussy throbbed harder and faster. Arousal swept over her as her body begged for him to be inside her.

"I want you too, Erik. I want you now," she moaned, breathless. "I need you."

He then slid off his shirt and placed it behind her on the countertop. He then lifted her up and propped her on the shirt so that her skin was comfortable.

He continued to kiss her hungrily then he lowered himself to her breasts. One hand caressed one of her breasts while he held her with his other hand. His lips brushed over her other breast then captured her taut nipple. He stroked his wet tongue over her hard pink nipple as she moaned with pleasure.

Soon he lowered himself to her wet folds between her legs.

She spread her legs wide on the countertop feeling her wetness between her legs. Soon his tongue was sliding between her folds and she jolted with heat and excitement. The feeling was so good, so amazing.

She held unto his head as he continued to pleasure her between her legs. Breathing heavy as his tongue swept in and out of her, she spasmed with a sweet orgasm she'd never felt before. He was so amazing.

"You like that, beautiful," he groaned as he moved up to her lips and kissed her. She tasted her own arousal on his lips.

"Yes, you feel so amazing, Erik," she whispered as he grinned with approval.

He then inched into her.

"I want to see you come again," he said, kissing her.

Before long, he'd reached into his pocket for a condom.

She was so glad he was prepared.

She grinned naughtily as she held unto him. Her arms wrapped behind his neck as she kissed him passionately. She then sucked on the side of his neck. He groaned with delight. She then moved her hands down to his buckle and undid his belt. Soon, she unzipped his zipper. He groaned with approval.

She helped him by removing his pants and silk boxers.

Her eyes widened with delight as she eyed his enormous erection.

"You're huge," she said with delight. He was big. His cock was huge, framed by a silky dusting of hair. His muscular pelvic region so well sculpted.

A surge of heat rushed through her as he rolled on his condom. She couldn't wait for him to be inside her.

Soon he leaned into her, his skin pressing against hers as she enjoyed the warm feel of his muscular body on hers. This was so erotic. So sensuous as they embraced, naked in the kitchen, bodies sweating from the heat of their passion.

She'd heard of heat in the kitchen but never had she ever thought she would experience *this* kind of heat.

She sucked on his lips as he lined up his erection to her opening.

Soon, he slowly slid his dick inside her small opening gently as she gasped with delight. He was so enormous as he filled her, stretching her softly as she tightened around his hard shaft. He then slowly pulled back out and she quivered with passion, wanting him to fill her again.

He thrust in and out of her slowly enjoying the feeling. Then he moved deeper inside her and moved back and forth, harder then faster as she groaned with delight begging him for more. They rocked back and forth fucking on the countertop until she came hard, her body shaking, orgasm rippling through her body. Erik came soon after as she shuddered with orgasmic release. Breathing hard and fast, they kissed passionately before collapsing into each other's arms. Sated and pleasured.

She'd never experienced lovemaking like that before.

She'd only agreed to one night with him. But she wanted more of Erik. So what were they going to do now? She didn't want to be without him. Ever.

Chapter 7 - Erik

Damn, Erik thought to himself the next morning with a warm smile curling his lips. He couldn't remember the last time he'd smiled that way.

He was in love. Undeniably in love. He cherished every inch of his beautiful friend, Candi. But she told him she only wanted just the one night. And he had to respect that.

But was he crazy? He didn't want to ever let her go. Ever.

He wanted to claim her for himself, to cherish and take care of her, provide for her, love her, every moment of her life.

He knew right then and there she was the one.

He turned and watched as she slept and wondered what was on her mind.

Just then, her pretty brown eyes pried open.

She looked like a curvy goddess. An earth angel beside him. He wanted to do everything in his power to give her everything she desired in life. Everything.

"You okay, beautiful?"

"Yes, thank you."

"Slept well?"

"I did. Did you."

"I sure did."

He surveyed her beautiful features, but there was something wrong. He could sense it.

"What's on your mind, princess?"

She propped herself up. "I want to thank you for helping me yesterday."

"Hey, it was no trouble. Glad I was in the area."

"Me too. It's not just with my car. Thanks for helping me with the storm."

"We all have fears."

"Do you?"

He grinned.

"None worth mentioning right now." He paused for a moment. "What else is on your mind, beautiful."

He surveyed her features, her pretty lips that brought him pleasure last night and her curvy body that he pleasured.

"I don't want to give you the wrong impression. About last night."

"The wrong impression? What do you mean by that?"

"I don't usually move so fast."

"Hey, we've known each other a while now. It's not like we just met."

"I know."

"But...?" he probed her, gently.

"But I promised myself I wouldn't date right now. Even though you tick all the boxes on my wish list."

"Your wish list?"

Her beautiful cheeks flushed.

"Oh, it's nothing. My girls and I have our wish list of what we want in a guy. I'm sure you guys have one too."

"Actually, most guys just want one thing." A sheepish grin slid on his lips as he combed his fingers through his after-sex wild hair.

"Do *you*?"

"I want more. I want a family. I didn't know it until last night. Like I said, after my ex left, I thought that was it for me. Until last night. I hope we can start something beautiful together. I don't mind committing to the right lady. I never felt this way about any woman before you."

He noticed her pretty lips parted in surprise. What was this gorgeous curvy goddess thinking? Did he say something wrong?

Chapter 8 – Candi

Commitment?

Did he just say commitment? Did he just admit he would love to see where this could go? Her ex was a commitment-phobic. But not Erik.

Commitment was *huge* on her boyfriend wish list.

Excitement rushed through her. She not only felt a sweet and strong chemistry with Erik and a connection that was indescribable, but she also loved that he wanted to have a wife and family one day. Most guys she'd met weren't ready or even thinking of that stuff.

"You really want a family one day?" she asked to be sure she heard right.

"Yes," he grinned sexily, "a wife to cherish and a family to love."

A grin curved her lips. Her heart galloped in her chest.

Yep, Erik ticked all the right boxes on her boyfriend wish list. She would be crazy not to go for it.

"I would love to have a future with you, Candi. I know we've only known each other casually, but last night was the best night of my life. I can't think of being with anyone but you. I've never felt a stronger connection. I guess it's true. When you meet the one, you just know it."

She leaned over to him and wrapped her arms around him.

He hugged her back warmly.

"Will you go to my brother's wedding with me?" he added.

"I would love to. And I know your brother will be thrilled to see you there. What changed your mind?"

"You did." He grinned.

"*I* did?"

"Yes, and your beautiful flowers are nothing compared to the beauty in your soul. I come alive around you."

"I feel the same way about you, Erik."

"I'd love to see where this goes."

"Same here."

"It reminds me of a saying I use to pin to my mirror."

"Which one is that?"

"*A flower cannot blossom without sunshine, and man cannot live without love* by Max Muller."

Her heart melted with joy and appreciation.

"You know that's my favorite quote too."

They had so much in common and yes, he ticked all the right boxes.

He leaned down and brushed his lips against hers, capturing her taste and pleasuring her with his lips.

"What a kiss," she said.

"That's to seal the deal, sweetheart. Let's do this."

"Are you sure?"

"Yes, I'm sure."

A warm smile curved her lips. "I would love that. Yes, let's start something beautiful," she said. And for the first time, she felt as if she was right where she belonged. In Erik's loving arms.

Thank you for reading *Claimed by the Mountain Man*. Available now – *Stranded with the Mountain Man* by Ann Ric.

Books by Ann Ric

Mountain Men of Charming Falls

Rescued by the Mountain Man (Evie & Jake)
Claimed by the Mountain Man (Candi & Erik)
Stranded with the Mountain Man (Lilly & Alex)
Christmas with the Mountain Man (Harmony & Chase)

Magic Protector Reverse Harem Trilogy

Magic Protector – A Steamy Paranormal Reverse Harem Romance (Book 1)
Magic Bound – A Steamy Paranormal Reverse Harem Romance (Book 2)
Magic Promise – A Steamy Paranormal Reverse Harem Romance (Book 3)

ABOUT THE AUTHOR

Ann Ric enjoys writing steamy paranormal romance novels and sizzling hot contemporary romance short stories with a happily ever after. She loves to read romance novels featuring strong characters and breathtaking worlds. You can reach her by email at heartandsoulbooks7@gmail.com